# VINCENT BANVILLE

## AN ACCIDENT WAITING TO HAPPEN

Vincent Banville is a writer, critic and journalist living in Dublin. His first novel, *An End to Flight*, won the Robert Pitman Literary Prize. He is also the author of five children's books, the *Hennessy* series, along with three crime novels, *Death by Design*, *Death the Pale Rider* and *Cannon Law* (New Island, 2001). He is the *Irish Times* crime critic.

GEMMA
*Open Door*

An Accident Waiting to Happen
First published by GemmaMedia in 2009.

GemmaMedia
230 Commercial Street
Boston MA 02109 USA
617 938 9833
*www.gemmamedia.com*



This edition of *An Accident Waiting to Happen* is published by arrangement with New Island Books Ltd.



Printed in the United States of America
Cover design by Artmark

13 12 11 10 09 1 2 3 4 5

ISBN: 978-1-934848-15-9

Library of Congress Preassigned Control Number (PCN) applied for

## OPEN DOOR SERIES

An innovative program of original
works by some of our most
beloved modern writers and
important new voices. First designed
to enhance adult literacy in Ireland,
these books affirm the truth that
a story doesn't have
to be big to open the world.

Patricia Scanlan
Series Editor

*For Aoife*
*Who has brought so much love*
*into all our lives*

# Chapter One

It was a raw, grey day in Dublin City. I had woken up that morning to find my two-year-old daughter Emily sitting on my chest. She was singing 'Twinkle, Twinkle, Little Star', only breaking off to demand to have her nappy changed. I did the necessary, then we went downstairs in search of something to eat.

We were in the sitting room, watching the Teletubbies and eating rice crispies, when my wife Annie came down. She has red hair and a temper to match. She also has definite views on how Emily should be brought up.

Now shaking her head, she said, 'What did I tell you? No television, no comfort food. You'll have the child spoiled. If we don't train her in before she comes to the age of reason —'

'Train her in?' I cut in. 'Why can't we let her be a free spirit? Do her own thing.'

'At the age of two?'

'Well, she can walk and talk. Sing, dance, say her abc's. I know she sometimes puts her shoes on the wrong feet, but that can happen to anyone.'

Annie's sense of humour will always overcome mock anger. Laughing, she bent down and planted a kiss on Emily's cheek. As she straightened up, I said, 'What about me?'

'What about you?'

'A kiss for Daddy?'

Thinking I was talking to her, Emily gave me a big wet, slushy one. I also got a mouthful of rice crispies, which went snap, crackle and pop.

After we were washed, cleaned and dressed, Annie took off for work, leaving me to drop Emily at her crèche. Rain was pouring down from an October sky, the clouds low and sulky. The kids in the crèche were in bad form too. Emily's friend Aoife attached herself to my leg like a limpet. She had to be removed with much wailing and gnashing of teeth. I felt for the carers, two young girls who couldn't be long out of their teens themselves.

My name is John Blaine, and I'm a private detective. What that means is that I stick my nose into people's business because other people pay me to do so. I find missing sons, daughters, wives and lovers. I spy with my little eye for folk involved in divorce cases. Once upon a time I worked for an insurance company, and a friend there, Tom Hardy, sometimes hires me to look into suspect claims. I'm good at my job, mainly because I'm six foot two, have scars on my face from my days on the Wexford hurling team, and am as stubborn as an old mule with a thorn up his bottom.

My office is located just off O'Connell Street. Down a lane behind the Imperial Hotel. The rain was still pelting down, drumming off a line of evil-smelling dustbins. I had to move one in order to get in my door. Up the stairs, into my outer office and through to the inner one. There was a musty smell, but I couldn't open a window for the very good reason that there wasn't one.

I looked through my mail, then

dumped most of it in the bin. My answering machine was more promising. A voice told me it was Bertie Boyer calling, the owner of the Purple Pussy nightclub. He might have some work for me if I cared to look in on him. He left a telephone number, then clicked off.

I rang the number, and waited until a very nice female voice said that she was Gertie and asked what she could do for me. I said I could think of quite a few things she could do for me, but for the moment it would be enough if she would put Bertie on the line. Bertie and Gertie, I mused, I wonder if they're related.

Bertie came on the line. He had a strong Dublin accent. He told me he couldn't talk over the phone, but if I dropped over he'd fill me in on what he wanted. The address of the club was in

Temple Bar, on the other side of the River Liffey. As I wasn't exactly snowed under with work, I told him I'd be over before noon.

I left soon after that, but I had only gone halfway up the lane when the wind blew my umbrella inside out. I dumped it and had to walk the rest of the way in the pelting rain. A bad start to the day, and it was about to get much worse.

# Chapter Two

The Temple Bar area prides itself on being Dublin's latest in-spot. It has a lot of trendy restaurants, trendy places to be seen, and trendy people to be heard. On this wet and windy October Thursday it was just as miserable as the rest of the city. Cold grey buildings, the smell of fast food, rubbish in the gutters. And one lonely street musician playing a sad song on his wailing violin.

The Purple Pussy nightclub was located in a narrow alley, which led down to the river. I recognised it because of the cut-out purple cat over the door. This appeared to be made of some type of light wood that swung in the wind. It was out-lined in neon strips, some of which had passed their sell-by date.

I knocked on the metal door and waited. A snake of water splashed down from a broken gutter and I had to be quick on my feet to avoid it. After two more knocks and a couple of kicks to the panel, a window opened above me and a head emerged.

'What's all the racket about?' a voice asked. 'We don't open till eleven tonight.'

I made the mistake of gazing upwards and got a splash of water in the face for my trouble. I moved back to get a better view. The face above me was young, female and nestled in a huge mop of bright blue hair. She didn't look very happy to see me.

'I'm John Blaine,' I bawled up at her. 'I was sent for. By Bertie. About a bit of business.'

'A bit of wha'?'

I sighed deeply, but resisted the temptation to throw something at her.

'Listen,' I said. 'Could you open the door and let me in? It's raining cats and dogs out here. And I'm not wearing my waterproof head.'

'Waterproof head. That's a good one. Hold on and I'll come down.'

I held on, and in a short while the door opened and I was invited inside. The head I had been talking to was now attached to a shapely body. She was dressed — but only just — in a halter-neck top and a skimpy pair of shorts. These garments were also in a fetching shade of blue. I gazed about me at the large barn-like building. The walls, drapes, tables, chairs and floor were all coloured purple. I had entered into a purple world.

We gazed at one another, the girl and me. She put a hand on her hip, then ran her tongue along her full lower lip. I shook the rain out of my hair like a wet dog, and tried to look neat, clean and well-advised.

'Bertie?' I hinted, hoping she hadn't gone into a coma on me.

'He's out the back.'

'The back?'

'That's where his office is. Through the bead curtain. Second door on the left.'

'Are you Gertie?'

'Who wants to know?'

'I told you. The name's John Blaine.'

'And you do what?'

'I sell purple paint. I thought you might be in the market for some.'

The girl giggled, then pushed at

me playfully with a hand that sported — yes, you've guessed it — purple nails.

'You're very tall,' she said. 'Where'd you get all them scars on your face?'

'Sticking it into other people's business. I'm a real Keyhole Kate.'

This time she gave a full-throated laugh. The halter-neck top groaned with the effort of keeping in her chest. I thought about making her laugh some more, but then remembered Bertie waiting for me in his office.

'I better get going,' I told her, rolling my eyes regretfully.

She nodded, then said, 'Gertie is the boss's other half. She's spoken for. I'm Denise and I'm free, white and over 21. Come up and see me sometime.'

'So that we can peel a grape together?'

'Something like that.'

# Chapter Three

The bead curtain clicked merrily as I went through it. Out of curiosity I peered into the first room on the left. It was a broom cupboard, containing brushes, and a battered-looking Hoover. Moving on, I knocked on the second door. I heard movement inside, so I turned the knob and went in.

A very large woman was sitting on a sofa opposite me. She was wearing a tent-like robe that covered her from her neck to her feet. Her hair was drawn back tightly into a bun, giving the skin of her face a stretched look. She was eating yoghurt from a tub, spooning it greedily into the cavern of her mouth. She paused when she saw me, then glanced to her right.

I followed her gaze and saw a tiny man sitting behind a huge desk. It was hard to judge, because he was sitting down, but he couldn't have been more than five feet in height. He had a mass of greying hair, cruel little eyes and a curl to his mouth that said mess with me and you'll be very sorry indeed. He was wearing a pinstripe grey suit and a dark blue shirt and tie. He had a little moustache under his nose that looked as if a centipede had crawled there and died. I took an instant dislike to him.

'Who the hell are you?' the little guy asked me, in a surprisingly deep voice.

Deciding not to take offence at his tone, I said mildly, 'I'm Blaine. You rang. Said you had something that might interest me.'

'Blaine, Blaine ...' He looked over at the woman on the sofa. 'You know anything about a Blaine, Gertie?'

Gertie shovelled in another spoonful of yoghurt, then let the tub rest on her mound of stomach. 'He's the private dick,' she told Tiny Tim. 'You found him in the Yellow Pages.'

'I take it you're Bertie Boyer,' I said, moving to stand in front of the desk. 'Owner of the Purple Pussy nightclub and husband of Gertie here.'

'Husband?' Gertie said. 'That's one for the birds. When are you going to make an honest woman of me, anyway, you little squirt? We've been engaged now since Jesus was a lad.'

'There's a time and a place to discuss that,' Boyer told her sourly. 'And it's definitely not now. Why don't you take your fat backside out of here and go help Denise get the place ready for tonight?'

'Why don't you go and take a running jump? Preferably off the side of a cliff. And you know Denise and me are not talking. Ever since I found the two of you together in here the night before last.'

'I've told you, we were discussing the stock market —'

'With your arm around her and your tongue stuck in her ear?'

Getting fed up with this family argument, I broke in. 'I'd love to stand here and do referee, but I have some other business to attend to. Maybe you could continue this later and in the meantime fill me in on whatever it is you want me to do?'

They glared at one another. Finally Gertie shoved herself off the sofa and padded out the door. A hippopotamus couldn't have done it more gracefully.

'Women,' Boyer muttered, shaking his head. I waited hopefully to see if the centipede moustache would fall off, but it stayed attached. He waved a hand at a straight-backed chair. 'Take the weight off your feet,' he said. 'I don't like people looking down at me.'

I did as I was bid, the chair creaking slightly as I planted myself in it. Then I sat back to listen to Bertie Boyer's tale of woe.

# Chapter Four

'I run a very popular joint here,' Bertie stated. 'We get all sorts coming to let their hair down. Doctors, lawyers, judges. Even some members of the government ...'

'I've heard the Taoiseach and the President have been seen dancing here together,' I said drily.

Bertie gave me a dirty look.

'If you don't believe me, come around tonight and see for yourself. The place'll be jumping.'

'I'm afraid I'm past all that. A family man, don't you know. With responsibilities. And in a very short time I have to pick up my baby daughter from her crèche. So I'd be grateful if you'd get the finger out and tell me what you want me to do.'

For a moment Bertie looked as if he was about to jump across the desk and catch me by the throat. But he thought better of it, and instead said, 'Are you into the strong-arm stuff? You look as if you've mixed it a bit in the past. That's a pretty lived-in face you're wearing.'

'I only use it during the day to scare off muggers. I've a much better-looking one for night-time.

'Yeah. Well, the thing is that I've got a problem with some hard cases who are demanding protection money from me. They say if I don't pay up they'll torch the place, with me ending up as burnt toast.'

'And Gertie the marmalade to go on it?'

'Whatever.'

I crossed my legs and leaned back. Normally I wouldn't touch something like this with a forty-foot pole. But I was badly in need of some readies and there wasn't any other work on the horizon.

'What exactly d'you want me to do?' I asked. 'I'll tough it out if I have to, but only after I've tried talking the other fellow to sleep first.'

'Well, that's exactly what I want you to do. Go and talk to these guys. Reason with them. And then when they can't see reason, beat the crap out of them with a baseball bat.'

'I haven't got a baseball bat. Would a hurley stick do?'

'Whatever.'

'Who are they?'

Bertie squinted his little eyes and tried not to look sly.

'They're a new breed of tough guys. Russkies or Bosnians or something like that. They don't talk the King's English.'

'You're telling me that some people from Eastern Europe are threatening to burn down your nightclub if you don't give them money?'

'That's exactly what I'm telling you. It's bad enough having to deal with the local hoodlums, but this new breed. I ask you ...'

'And you want me to go and talk them out of their plans?'

'I'll pay you well. Two hundred now, and another three hundred if you get them off my back. Can't say fairer than that, can I?'

'I keep the two hundred whether I succeed or not?'

'You'll have to bring back some proof that you went. Maybe a finger or a toe. Or you could scalp one of them. They're into long hair.'

I rubbed my face and thought about it. I had nothing to lose by going to see these people, and I badly needed the two hundred quid. There wasn't much chance that I'd get them to back off, but one never knew.

'Okay,' I said, leaning forward. 'Tell me where these guys live and I'll pay them a visit. But I can't promise anything.'

'That's all I ask,' Bertie said, doing his best to look sincere.

He opened a drawer in the desk and fumbled about in it. He finally took out a wad of money held together by a rubber band. Snapping off four fifties, he slid them across to me. He also gave me a sheet of paper with a name and address on it. That finished our little family gathering for the moment, so I got up and left. There was no sign of either of the girls as I moved across the dance floor towards the door.

# Chapter Five

I went back out into the rain. Knitting needles of it were dancing on the pavement. At two I would have to collect Emily from the crèche. It was now twelve-thirty. Sheltering in a shop doorway, I examined the note Bertie Boyer had given me. The name on it was Polonski. The address was down in Parnell Street.

My car, a very old Renault, was once again in the garage. A taxi? A bus? I decided to walk. A guy in a plastic raincoat, carrying a large golf umbrella gave me shelter as far as Eason's bookshop. From there on it was water, water everywhere. By the time I got to the Polonski address, I was wet through.

Number 49A was a fast-food joint. It was closed but still encased in the tangy smell of last night's fish and chip dinners. Shading my eyes with my hands, I gazed in through the glass. No sign of life. There was a door in an alcove beside the shop. I pressed the bell and waited. After a time I heard movement inside, then the door suddenly opened and a large dog came bounding out.

It was a labrador. Now labradors are usually placid dogs, but this fellow appeared quite annoyed about something. And he looked as if he were blaming me for the cause of his annoyance. He approached me slowly, a growl deep in his throat. I placed my hands over my essentials, like a football defender awaiting a Beckham free kick. It's a well-known fact that a dog knows when someone is scared. It was my hope that the smell from the fish and chip shop might distract him from the waves of fear washing over me. It didn't seem like it, though.

I was about to turn on my heel and run when an old woman appeared in the doorway behind him. She said something in a language foreign to my ear and the dog suddenly paused. He cocked his head to one side, gave a whine, then began to backtrack. I could have kissed that old lady.

She now turned to me and asked what I wanted. Dressed all in black, she looked to be in mourning for some departed relative. Her skin was stained brown as if she had spent some time in a smoke house. A plait of grey hair hung down her back like a bell rope.

'The Polonski residence?' I inquired, still keeping a fearful eye on the labrador. 'Are you the woman of the house?'

'You say?'

'I need to speak with a Polonski. Is your husband, uncle, son, any male member of the family at home?'

'Whatever you're selling, we don't need it.'

'I'm not trying to sell you anything.'

'You're from the corporation?'

'No to that too. I've come to inspect the house for cockroaches. There's an outbreak of them in the area.'

This really confused her. It appeared to confuse the dog too, for he advanced and began growling again. I decided to give up and try again another, sunnier, day. As I turned on my heel, a man loomed up behind the old lady and gave me the eye.

He was a sturdy looking guy. Middle-aged, he had a grey crew-cut, a huge moustache and watchful eyes. He was wearing overalls and wellington boots, and he carried a workman's tool box in his right hand.

'You're Mr Polonski?' I asked, even daring to take a step forward.

'What you want to know for?'

I took a card out of my wallet and offered it to him. Immediately the labrador jumped up and snapped it from between my fingers. Then he sat down on his hind legs and began tearing it to pieces.

'My name is John Blaine,' I said, trying again. 'I've been sent by Bertie Boyer, the owner of the Purple Pussy nightclub. He feels we might have something to discuss.'

'You've brought my money?'

'What money?' I said, quickly putting my wallet back in my pocket.

'The money that man owes me. For work done.'

I thought about that, then I said, 'I wonder if I could come in for a minute? Out of the rain.'

The man looked undecided. He said something to the old lady in her own language. They muttered together for a few moments. The dog had finished eating my card, but he still looked hungry. I was starting to wonder if my coming here was such a good idea when the man gestured to me to come in. If I did so I would be out of the rain, but would I be safe from the dog? Only time would tell.

# Chapter Six

We climbed a stairs, the old lady, the dog, me, and the male Polonski taking up the rear. A right turn and we were in a large room that smelled faintly of exotic food. Curries? Chicken tikka? Bacon and cabbage? There was a lot of solid-looking furniture, and gilt hangings on the walls. On the floor lay a blue rug with images of wild animals eating each other on it. Dotted about were lots of statues and paintings of foreign-looking saints. It appeared as if the Polonskis had transferred a bit of their homeland to dear old Ireland.

Without being asked, I sat down on a cushioned chair as far away from the dog as I could get. The old lady chose a sofa and seemed instantly to go to sleep. I would have given anything for a cigarette, but I was in the process of giving them up. No passive smoking for daughter Emily. Orders from Captain Annie, she who must be obeyed.

'You are Mr Polonski?' I asked the guy in the wellington boots. 'I wouldn't want to be talking to the wrong man.'

'Abraham Polonski,' came the answer, said with no little pride. 'Why have you come here, if it is not to bring me my money?'

He placed his toolbox on the rug, sat down and began to roll a cigarette. I wondered if I asked him politely would he roll one for me too.

'You know trying to get that kind of

money is against the law,' I told him. 'Surely it's the same in your country?'

'My country?' He curled his lip and looked as if he were about to spit. 'Ireland is my country now. I have been here for five years. My family is also here.'

'Well then, all the more reason why you shouldn't go around threatening people.'

'Threatening people? What people?'

'Bertie Boyer, for starters.'

'That man!' — Again he looked as if he'd like to spit — 'I did all that work for him and now he refuses to pay me.'

The dog had sat up and was taking notice, so I said hastily, 'I didn't know you'd done work for him. He told me you were threatening to burn down his nightclub if he didn't pay you protection money.'

Polonski finished rolling his

cigarette and stuck it in his mouth. There was a large silver teapot standing on a small gas jet near him. He found a bit of paper, stuck it in the jet and, when it took fire, used it to light his cigarette. He paused, the burning paper still in his hand.

'It is true I suggested I might set fire to his place, but it was said in the heat of anger. He employed me to redecorate the club. Myself and my son laboured over the job for a month. If you've been there you can see what a good job we did. He owes me five thousand euro, but he keeps telling me he has a cash-flow problem. Can you blame me for losing my temper with him?'

I got up, but when the dog growled I sat down again. Rain beat against the high windows of the room and it was beginning to get dark. But not as dark as the thoughts in my head. It was obvious that someone was lying, either Bertie Boyer or Mr Abraham Polonski. But which one? Was Bertie hoping the sight of my ugly face would persuade Polonski to give up seeking what was rightly his? Or was Polonski hiding his dirty work under the disguise of real work done? I'd need the wisdom of Solomon to come up with the right answer here.

# Chapter Seven

It was still only early afternoon, yet the room was getting darker and darker. I remembered Emily in the crèche and the fact that it was my turn to pick her up.

'I'll have to get back to you about this business,' I told Polonski. 'There are two different versions of the story and I'll have to look into them. If Boyer does owe you money, there are legal ways of going about getting it from him.'

'Legal, hah!' Polonski drew on his cigarette, then blew smoke at the ceiling. 'My ancestors were Romanian gypsies, Mr Blaine. A proud people. In days gone by we settled our disagreements in the fire of battle. I understand that things are different in Ireland, but some of the young people cling to the old ways. I have a son, and sometimes it is not easy for him to hold in his temper. Each day we go out on the streets we are abused. We are told that we are not welcome here, and that we should go back to our own country. Only recently were we allowed to work. It is difficult ...'

'I understand that,' I said. 'But you still can't go around threatening to burn down people's nightclubs. Even if the owners do owe you money. I only came here to reason with you, not to bully you.'

Again I stood up, and again the dog arose, his teeth bared and a growl echoing in his throat. Polonski muttered something at him. Then he turned to me. 'Tell Boyer he must give me my money. It is only just that he pay for work done. Then there will be no anger between us.'

I nodded, then headed for the stairs. I was halfway down when the door below burst open. A young man with wet curly hair, wearing overalls similar to Polonski's, came in. He looked up at me, and the expression on his face was not exactly one of friendship.

'Who're you?' he asked, advancing up a couple of steps.

'The name is Blaine,' I answered. Then, choosing my words carefully, I said, 'I've some business with Mr Polonski. I take it you're his son?'

'I am. What kind of business?'

Behind me, the elder Polonski made soothing noises, then said, 'Don't do anything rash, Leo. We don't want trouble.'

'Trouble? Are we not drowning in trouble? In Romania. In every country we've gone to since we left there. And now here. It is time we stood up for ourselves. Give trouble, instead of taking it.'

'Listen to your father, Leo,' I advised him, going down some more steps until we were standing face to face. 'Breaking the law will get you nowhere, except maybe a prison term.'

'Don't call me Leo,' the young man said, thrusting his face up against mine. 'My given name is Leck, and I'm proud of it. And who are you anyway?'

'Just a messenger.'

'Who from?'

'Bertie Boyer. He says your family have made threats against his property.'

'He owes us money and refuses to pay us.'

'So why don't you send him a solicitor's letter?'

'That kind of man would merely wipe his backside with it. He only understands one kind of action.'

'The violent kind?'

'Exactly.'

'Let me talk to him. Maybe I can make him see sense.'

'Do you work for him?'

'Only since this morning. And I have a feeling that by this evening I won't be working for him any more.'

Young Polonski stood aside, still looking sulky, and I went past him and out the door. It banged shut behind me, leaving me once more in the rain. And it was coming down harder than ever.

## Chapter Eight

I got a taxi to the garage on the North Circular Road and persuaded the owner, Alfie, to give me back my car. It is an old Renault 9 that should have been pensioned off years ago. Alfie told me the engine block was about to split and that it was gulping down oil by the gallon.

I took it anyway, but had only got as far as the Mater Hospital when the car gave a death rattle and died. Maybe it was the sight of the hospital that did it. I told the Sergeant on duty in Mountjoy Garda station about it. He surprised me by saying he'd have it towed into the pound where they kept stolen vehicles. He must have been in a good mood that day.

I walked up to the crèche and collected Emily. She was wearing a plastic rain hat and someone else's coat. We sorted that out, then one of the girls kindly rang for a taxi for me. I wondered why everyone was being so nice, and put it down to the fact that I looked like a drowned rat.

Emily and myself headed out to Clontarf to Annie's mother's house. Elsie, the mother, has little time for me. She believes that her daughter married beneath her when she took me as her other half. And my bouts of binge drinking have confirmed her in her view.

She's a widow, living alone except for a pug dog named Mary O'Leary.

This in spite of the fact that it's a male. The dog has no time for me either. He shows this by lying at my feet when I'm in the house and farting into my face.

I asked the taxi driver to wait, then went up the path to the house and rang the bell. Elsie has a fear of someone breaking in and interfering with her, so she's had an intercom installed. Her voice boomed out of this, asking who was there.

'It's your favourite son-in-law,' I told the black box on the door frame.

'Which one?'

'You've only got one. Will you open the door and stop messing about?'

'Are you sober?'

'Yes I'm sober. I've been off the drink for months.'

'How do I know that?'

'Smell my breath through the box?'

'Don't be ridiculous. Is Emily with you?'

'No, I've put her out on the streets to sell her body. Of course she's with me. Don't you take care of her every day at this time? Now, will you open the door? We're getting wet out here.'

The buzzer buzzed and I pushed the door. I sent Emily in first in order to calm Mary O'Leary. When he's excited he farts worse than ever. We went into the kitchen, where Annie's mother was standing at the table, her hands covered in flour. That's how she puts in most of her time, baking. She lives on a road of fat people, all of them bullied into eating Elsie's chocolate cakes, jam rolls and apple tarts.

The dog flap banged back and Mary O'Leary ran in, wearing a raincoat and a little three cornered hat. He screeched to a halt when he saw me. Then he veered over to Emily, rolled on his back and waited to have his belly scratched. The sight made me feel sick to my stomach.

Elsie is a small stick of a woman with permed hair and a glare that would burn a hole in metal. When I'm around she always seems about to come to the boil. I eyed the wooden spoon in her hand and kept my distance.

'Annie will pick her up as usual?' she now asked me.

'Yes. Around four.'

'You'll be working?' This was said in a tone that hinted at the fact that she believed I had never worked a day in my life.

I thought I'd really give her something to get her teeth into, so I said, 'No, we both live on Annie's salary. I'm going off drinking with my mates. Work is a four letter word as far as I'm concerned.'

I could see her thinking seriously about running around the table and giving me a belt with the wooden spoon. Before she could make up her mind I bent and kissed Emily, then made my getaway. God help the batter in the bowl, it was in for a terrible beating.

# Chapter Nine

I went back to my office. It was as empty as the last time I'd been there. Taking off my outer clothes, I hung them on the single radiator to dry. There was soon a damp, clothes-drying smell in the room you could cut with a knife.

I sat at the desk in my underwear and rang George Quinlan. George is a superintendent in the Garda Siochana. Some years ago we had both been in a gun club together. We had got to know each other a little. In more recent times my business as a private snoop had led me into his terrain. I had helped to put a few thugs behind bars, something that caused George to be a little less frosty towards me.

He was busy on another line, but the sergeant who answered said he'd have him ring me back. I stared at the opposite wall for a while, then bent down and opened the bottom drawer of the desk. That's where I keep the office bottle of Bushmills whiskey.

I was wet, cold and feeling miserable. Surely I deserved a small snort? I shook the bottle and watched the amber liquid slosh about. I could swear it winked at me. There was a shot glass in the drawer also, and I filled this to the brim. I placed it on the blotter in front of me. Forbidden fruit? Most definitely.

The first sip went down like molten gold. I was about to send down a second to keep it company when the phone rang. Feeling guilty, I picked it up, hoping it wasn't Annie. She'd be able to smell the drink even down the line. But I was saved: it was George Quinlan.

'Blaine? I hope this is important. I'm very busy at the moment.'

'Making out your expense sheet for the week?'

'Now that's the kind of remark that gets people's backs up. What is it about you? Always the smart alec.'

'I'm sorry, George. I've been out in the rain and I think it's softened my brain. I know how busy you are, so I'll be brief.'

'What is it, then?'

'What d'you know about a guy called Bertie Boyer? He's the owner of a nightclub in Temple Bar. It's called the Purple Pussy.'

There was a silence, during which I took the chance to knock back the rest of the whiskey. It went against my breath, causing me to cough into the phone. This brought George back to life.

'Why d'you want to know about him? Is he a friend of yours?'

'Not particularly. More a business connection.'

'Well, I wouldn't get involved with him, if I was you. I'd have to look up the files, but off the top of my head I'd say he's a shady character. I've heard him mentioned a few times around here.'

'In what context?'

'Oh, receiving stolen goods, turning a blind eye to the selling of drugs on his premises. He likes to be seen with heavy hitters from the gangster ranks.'

I thought about that for a few

seconds. I then asked, 'Just one other favour. Will you see if the records have anything on a Romanian family named Polonski? They might be involved in the protection business.'

I could hear George draw in his breath and I knew what was coming. I was right.

'Am I some kind of servant of yours? Is the whole police force to be at your beck and call? I've more to be doing than looking up information for you. Anyway, these people have a right to privacy ...'

'George, George, you know I wouldn't ask if it wasn't important. What are friends for?'

'I'm not your friend. You're merely someone I happen to know. And you're a bloody nuisance, most of the time.'

He went on like this for a while longer. But later in the afternoon he rang back to tell me there was no record of any wrong-doing by the members of the Polonski family.

It looked as if it was my client, the man I had taken money from, who was telling the lies and maybe setting me up. Now, why would he be doing that? I wondered.

# Chapter Ten

Home is where the heart is, so home I went. The rain was still coming down in bucketfuls. Some poet or other referred to rain as angels' tears. Well, they must be pretty sad up in heaven today, I thought as I sloshed up the Cabra Road.

I had a bath to try to warm up, then broke open a bale of briquettes and lit a fire in the sitting room. I was dozing in front of its warming breath when Annie and Emily came in. Neither of them was in a good mood. Before they could attack, I said, 'I've rung for a take-away. Beef in black bean sauce for the elder lemons, noodles for the kid. Sit down and toast your toes and I'll set the table.'

I escaped to the kitchen and began to make noise with plates and cutlery. The back yard was flooded again, so I drew the blind so that Annie wouldn't see it. She had been asking me to do something about it for months.

I was standing admiring the array on the table when my mobile phone began ringing. I clicked it on.

'Hello?'

'Blaine?'

'Speaking.'

'Bertie Boyer here. Did you get a result with those plonkers?'

'The Polonskis?'

'Whatever.'

'I did go to see them. But they gave

me a different version of how things stand than you did.'

'Well, they would, wouldn't they? You didn't think they'd put their hands up to threatening me just because you stuck your ugly mug in, did you?'

I took a deep breath and counted to three. To keep my temper, I promised myself I'd bite one of his ears off the next time I saw him.

As calmly as possible I said, 'They told me you owed them money. For work they did in the club. Painting and decorating and the like.'

'You've been here. You've seen what they did. Would you pay them? If I hadn't moved fast they'd have painted me purple. As well as the walls, the ceiling, the floor ...'

'You didn't tell them to do it that way?'

'I asked for something tasteful. A

little of this, a little of that. After all, it's a high-class joint.'

'I know, you've told me already. Only the beautiful and the best go there. But to get back to matters at hand, if you owe them you'll have to pay up. That's the way it works.'

'To hell with that. They've threatened to burn the place down. I want you down here tonight to keep an eye on things. I've paid you good money, now earn it.'

'My car's broken down.'

'Then get a taxi. Walk, run, crawl, but be here. We open for business at eleven. Maybe you'll strike it lucky with one of the girls. I doubt it though, with a kisser like yours.'

He rang off before I could come up with a suitable reply. I considered flinging the phone at the wall, but the thought of the expense of buying a new one stopped me. He was a nasty little git, but it was true that I'd taken his money. Unlike him, I believed in paying my debts.

The women of the house had thawed out in front of the fire. Annie was half asleep in an armchair, while Emily was doing her Winnie the Pooh jigsaw. I sat down on the floor beside her, but every time I tried to fit a piece she slapped my hand away. She had her mother's temper.

When the food arrived, we ate it straight from the containers. I opened a bottle of wine, and Emily drank black currant juice. I felt good, sitting there in the bosom of my family. But the rain continued beating on the window, and the knowledge that I'd have to go out in it later on kept me on edge. If I'd known what was in store for me, I'd have locked all the doors, drawn all the curtains and stayed indoors with my loved ones till morning.

# Chapter Eleven

At the weekend, Temple Bar is really jumping. To earn some extra money I sometimes do bouncer at one of the clubs. It is not an enjoyable experience. Stag and hen parties are the worst, the men looking for fights, the women loud and behaving in a most unladylike fashion.

This Thursday night, probably because of the rain, things were rather quiet. The street musician was still playing his violin outside the Purple Pussy. He was a tall thin guy with long hair and a scraggy beard. I dropped a pound coin into his tray and, when he grinned at me, he showed me purple gums and no teeth.

It was just coming up to twelve o'clock and a small queue had formed at the door. A burly individual with a shaved head stood with his back to the entrance. He let people in or kept them out as the mood took him. When I made to go past him, he placed a large hand on my chest and pushed me back.

'Where d'you think you're going?' he asked, squinting his eyes.

'I'm one of the male strip team,' I told him. 'The ladies inside can't wait to get their hands on my parts.'

He stood back and looked me up and down.

'Oh yeah? Well, I haven't been told nothing about this. Have you some kind of pass?'

'Pass? No pass. But you could ring Bertie on your mobile and tell him Blaine is here. He'll vouch for me.'

A change came over him when I mentioned Bertie's name. He gave me a grin only a little less horrible than the street musician's, and said, 'You know the boss? Why didn't you say so in the first place?'

'You didn't give me a chance.'

Again I started to go past him and again he put his hand out to stop me.

'What is it now?'

'I've often thought I could do that strippin' business,' he said. 'How d'you get into it?'

This time it was my turn to look him up and down.

'You've got to have a beautiful body for starters. Give me a call when you've lost a few pounds, had your nose straightened and your ears pinned back. And see if you can do something about those teeth, fill in the gaps maybe ...'

Before the penny dropped that I was having him on, I pushed past him and went inside. Dance music was making the walls bulge, and a number of couples were staggering about to its beat. I made for the bar. Denise was serving behind it, wearing spangles and a g-string. I ordered a club soda, then stood with my back to the counter and gazed around the room. Most of the people present were sitting at tables. They looked older than the usual types one saw in such places. I counted three guys in evening suits who could have been the doorman's brothers. They were standing about, trying to look as if they didn't work there.

Why hadn't Bertie sent a couple of them to warn off the Polonskis? I wondered. He already had them on a salary. Didn't make sense for him to pay me, when he had his own hard men already at hand. Probably the best way to find out would be to ask him.

I went towards the bead curtain that gave access to his office, but was again stopped in my tracks by one of the hired help. This guy had a crew cut and a chest like the side of a large building.

He said something to me that I couldn't hear above the din of the thumping music. Just at that moment, though, the curtain was pushed aside and Bertie's other half, Gertie, stuck her head out. She looked from one to the other of us, then nodded at the bouncer. He took his hand away and I followed Gertie on through and back in the direction of the office. She hadn't lost any weight since I'd last seen her. If there was a mud-wrestling contest for women, she'd win it hands down.

## Chapter Twelve

Bertie was sitting in the same chair behind the same desk. He was all done up in evening wear, white shirt gleaming, dicky bow poking out from under his chin. He reminded me of a ventriloquist's dummy.

Gertie placed herself in her usual position on the sofa. She had so many chins she appeared to have a ladder up to her face. I wondered if Bertie climbed it in order to give her a kiss.

'So,' he now said, 'what's up? Have you put those foreign guys in hospital yet? Or am I still to expect a visit from them tonight?'

'Tonight's the night?'

'Could be. The time for talking is well over.'

I sat down on the same chair I'd used that morning and crossed my legs. I adjusted the crease in my trousers, leaned back, wished I had a cigarette. All the while Bertie watched me, with a look on his face as if someone had placed a week-old mackerel under his nose.

'Who the hell asked you to sit down?' he demanded. 'You should be outside waiting for the Polookas to show up. With their cans of kerosene and their oily rags. We could all go up in flames and you'd still be here admiring the shine on your shoes.'

I gazed across at Gertie. She raised an eyebrow and made a face. It takes a lot for me to lose my temper, but I was pretty near breaking point at that moment. Controlling myself with an effort, I said, 'Why'd you hire me in the first place? You've a collection of goons working for you who'd do the job much better than me. I'd imagine they'd enjoy breaking bones and dishing out a few cuts and bruises.'

There was a fine silver box on Bertie's desk. He opened the lid of this and took out a cigar. It was long enough to poke a rat out from under a hedge. He bit off one end, then lit the other. Puffing manfully he blew out clouds of blue smoke. It was hard to know if he was smoking the cigar or the cigar was smoking him.

Through the smoke he said, 'Short of bringing the fuzz in on this, I wanted some kind of official action taken. You were the next best thing to the pigs. I could've sent my men over, but it's them that would've ended up in the slammer. You must have a licence of some kind ...'

'But it doesn't entitle me to beat people up.'

'Aw, I was only rattling your chain about that. All I wanted was for you to talk to them. Make them see sense. The rest was me having a little joke.'

'You really think they'll try to burn your place down?'

'Who knows?'

I watched him throw burning ash from his cigar on the floor, as if he meant to get in first and do the job himself. Gertie noticed it too.

She said, 'Will you watch what you're doing? There's an ashtray on the desk. Use it. For a little man you dirty up the place something awful.'

Throwing more ash on the floor,

Bertie said, 'Watch your mouth. You're getting a bit too cheeky lately.'

Gertie laughed.

'What are you going to do, put me across your knee and spank me?'

'You'd be so lucky.'

The vision of the huge Gertie lying across Bertie's little legs helped to banish my bad humour. I was feeling quite cheerful again as I stood up to go.

'Where're you off to now?' Bertie asked sourly.

'I'm going to do what you told me. Walk around and keep an eye out for fire bugs. That's what you paid me for and that's what I'm about to do. In the meantime, you'd better stick that cigar in a bucket of water. Otherwise you might do the job yourself and save the Polonskis the trouble.'

# Chapter Thirteen

I did stroll around for a while, giving Denise the eye and getting in the way of the bouncers. The only result of this was that I drank too much beer and got a pounding headache from the thundering music. None of the Polonski family showed up and the only trouble was caused by an elderly man who got drunk and threw up over one of the waitresses.

I signed off at three a.m. and went home. I couldn't get a taxi, so I walked. The rain had stopped and there was a backbone of stars down the length of the sky. In Phibsboro, St Peter's church was floodlit, but all its doors were closed and locked. No refuge there for someone in need.

Likewise my house on the Cabra road, closed and locked that is. I let myself in and crept up the stairs. The friendly ghost that also lived there kept pace with me as I climbed. Emily was in her cot, Annie in our big double bed. She groaned when I slipped in beside her, and slapped at my cold hand when I placed it on her bare shoulder.

I lay and listened to her gentle snoring, her breath fluttering against my face. This was where I liked to be, in bed with my beloved. And the wind had got up again and brought more rain, beating it against the window. What bliss to be inside, out of its reach.

But my bliss didn't last long. I was just sliding into sleep when the loud bleeping of my mobile phone hammered into the quiet room. Annie sat bolt upright, while Emily let out a roar that probably scared even the friendly ghost. Half falling out of bed, I crawled on my hands and knees to the chair over which I'd draped my jacket.

While Annie switched on the light and went to soothe Emily, I pressed the receive button. A voice with a slight foreign accent said, 'Blaine, is that you?'

'It is now, but when my wife gets her hands on me I'll be the late Blaine.'

'Pardon?'

'Never mind. What is it you want? And who are you, anyway?'

'It's Abraham Polonski. My son Leo is missing and I can't find him.'

'Maybe he's with Bo-Peep's sheep. Or living next door to Alice.'

'Alice?'

I gave Annie an I-can't-help-it look, then sat on the chair, cradling my chin on my hand.

'How long has Leo been missing?' I said into the phone. 'And why d'you feel I can help you find him?'

'I think he's been kidnapped by Bertie Boyer. You seemed to believe me today when you came to my house. Go to Boyer and tell him he can keep my money. Only give me back my son.'

'But why would he take your son in the first place?'

'Leo is not patient like me. Perhaps he went to Boyer and made more threats against him. Offered to do him harm.'

'He'd do that?'

'He has a temper. But he is not a bad boy. It's just that he gets frustrated.'

'And you're afraid Boyer and his thugs will try to teach him a lesson?'

'There is that possibility.'

Having met Boyer and his hard men I had to agree that he might be on the right track there. I remembered the long cigar and could imagine the damage it would do if the burning end were pressed against someone's face or neck.

'You'll go there and plead for my son's release?' the voice from the phone asked.

'To the nightclub?'

'Isn't that the most likely place to find them?'

'I suppose so.'

'Then it's settled. I wait to hear from you.'

The phone clicked off before I could agree or disagree. Another right mess you've got yourself into, I said into the now silent instrument. Although by the look on Annie's face, as she held the crying Emily, it was a good idea to get out of there as fast as possible.

# Chapter Fourteen

Once again I trudged through the rain, which was coming down as hard as ever. Along the Cabra Road onto the North Circular. Then by the Mater Hospital, its lighted windows like holes in the darkness of the night.

I had jammed one of Emily's plastic rain hats onto my head and was sporting a bright yellow cape. It was something like Clint Eastwood used to wear in those spaghetti westerns he made when he and I were much younger. As I passed along O'Connell Street, two drunks got a great laugh out of my appearance. 'Look, it's Big Bird,' they shouted, falling about the place.

I made it to Temple Bar and the front of the Purple Pussy nightclub. There was no sign of life. Even the busker with the fiddle had gone home to bed. I put my ear to the door and listened. All I could hear was the pitter-patter of the rain as it bounced off my plastic hat.

It was time to do a bit of exploring. I went around the side of the building, lighting my way with the flashlight I'd been wise enough to bring. More dustbins, and a large rat who looked quite put out at the fact that I'd disturbed him. There was a metal door, but it was securely locked. However, a window with a wire grille over it looked more promising.

After much pulling, dragging and swearing, I managed to prise the grille back far enough to see that the window was not fully closed. I got my fingers under it and pushed it far enough up to allow me to wriggle in. The flashlight showed me that I was in the corridor that led to Bertie Boyer's private quarters.

It was in darkness, so I had to be careful as I moved along it. There was a light under the door of Bertie's office. I went forward and put my ear to it. I could hear a murmur of voices, but couldn't make out anything that was being said.

What to do? Should I just barge in? Accuse Bertie of kidnapping young Leo Polonski and demand to have him sent back to his grieving father? Or should I adopt a softly-softly approach? Beat around the bush a bit before asking Bertie if he knew anything about the whereabouts of young Leo?

My problem was solved when the door suddenly opened and a guy with a cannonball for a head looked out at me. It was hard to say which of us was the more surprised. My first instinct was to turn and run for my life, but then I decided to brazen it out.

Bertie was again sitting behind his desk, looking more than ever like a midget with overblown ideas of his own importance. Gertie was on the sofa, this time eating a banana. There were two hard men in tuxedos, as well as the guy behind me breathing down my neck.

But it was the sight of Leo Polonski, sitting on a wooden chair in the middle of the room, which caught my attention. His hands were handcuffed behind him and he was slumped sideways, his head on his chest. There was a small pool of what looked like blood on the carpet beside the chair.

Gertie nearly choked on the banana when she saw me, while Bertie and the two hard men broke into guffaws of laughter. 'I know, I know, I look like Big Bird,' I said. 'I've been told that already.' Pointing at the silent Leo, I asked, 'Is he dead or only taking time out?'

'Don't worry about him,' Bertie said, when he'd got his breath back. 'He'll be all right after a few weeks in hospital. Why don't you come and sit down? We were just talking about you, as it happens. And now here you are, as large as life and twice as comical.'

I made to take off my cape and the guy behind me put his large hands on my shoulders.

'Keep it on,' he growled. 'You won't

be able to move around as fast with that thing on you.'

'Can I at least take off the hat?' I asked. 'It's squeezing my brains so much I can't think.'

'What d'you want to think for?' said Bertie. 'Look at Gertie there, she's never had a thought in her life and it hasn't done her any harm.'

Gertie gave him the finger, using the half-eaten banana. 'Up yours, squirt,' she said, before cramming the rest of the fruit into her mouth.

The guy with his hands on my shoulders moved me forward, and pushed me down onto a chair beside Leo Polonski. Then he stood back, but not too far that he couldn't catch hold of me if I tried to leap over the desk and bite Bertie's ear off. I prised Emily's hat off my head and held it in my lap. Maybe if things got really

rough I'd be able to use it as a weapon
and beat someone unconscious with it.

# Chapter Fifteen

'So,' Bertie said, like a chairman bringing a meeting to order. 'I didn't expect you to show up. What brought you here, anyway?'

'I had a call from Leo's father ...' I began, but was interrupted by a muffled sound from said Leo.

I leaned in close to him and asked, 'What's that you said?'

Slowly his head came up off his chest and I found myself gazing into a pair of bloodshot eyes.

'The name's Leck, not Leo,' he croaked. 'I've told you that already.'

'Sorry, sorry.'

I patted him on the shoulder, glad to see that he had enough spirit in him to worry about being given his proper name. If I'd been in his condition they could have called me Tilly the Dairy Maid and it wouldn't have bothered me.

While this was going on, Bertie had found another of his giant cigars and was in the process of lighting it. He got it going to his satisfaction and leaned back in his chair.

'The fact of your showing up means we'll have to change our plans,' he said.

'The sign of a good general,' I told him. 'Being able to think on his feet. What are these plans you're talking about?'

'You're not going to like them.'

'Tell me, anyway.'

He brought the chair forward,

narrowly missing hitting his chin off the desk.

'For a while now I've been planning to get out of the nightclub business and try something different. But I need money to get started. As I've got a bit of a cash flow problem, I thought it would be an idea to burn down this building and get the insurance money.'

'It never entered your head that doing such a thing is against the law?'

'Well now, there you've hit the nail on the head. In the past a number of my other properties just happened to catch fire. And I've put in a few claims in my time.'

'So, on this occasion you're going to blame it on someone else. And who better than a crowd of Romanian gypsies, who have only recently come to this country looking for refuge?'

'Exactly.'

'And where do I fit in? After all, you're not short of staff to carry out your orders.'

'I needed someone on the right side of the law. Someone who would testify that I'd been threatened by these blow-ins. You were to be my character witness.'

'And now I've gone and spoiled things by stumbling on your plan?'

'Not necessarily.'

Bertie placed his cigar in an ashtray big enough for him to take a bath in. I didn't like the look on his face as he opened a drawer in the desk and took out a tiny tape recorder. He switched it on and we were listening to a recording of our conversation of the day before, when he had hired me to go talk to the Polonski family.

Clicking off the machine, he said, 'Now, this is the way it is. The club burns down and the remains of two bodies are found. One is that of the guy who started the fire, the other the one trying to stop him. In fact, Polooka here and your very self. When the insurance tossers show up, I play them the tape. Bingo, they pay up and Bertie is rolling in the readies. Sweet as a nut, don't you think?'

I had to take a deep breath before I could answer. As a matter of fact, I had to take a number of deep breaths. And even then, the only thing that got up my nose was the smell of burning. It was probably coming from Bertie's cigar. But it could also have been a grim warning of what was to come.

# Chapter Sixteen

I decided the time had come for action, so I got up off the chair with the idea of then throwing it at Bertie. But Head-the-Ball behind me had been right when he'd stopped me from taking off the blasted cape. It hindered my movements no end.

Before I could do anything other than stand up, the guy had wrapped his arms around me in a bear hug. Then one of the other thugs approached and handcuffed my hands in front of me. I was put back on the chair, the two of them standing beside me like bookends.

'Are you sure this is such a good idea?' Gertie suddenly spoke up. She sounded worried.

'Yes, Bertie,' I chimed in. 'You're pushing up into the big league here. Ripping off the insurance company is one thing, but murder is quite another. If they get you for this, they'll lock you in the clink and throw away the key.'

'But they won't get me, will they? No one knows about it except the people here in this room. And they won't talk.'

'How can you be so sure?' I looked around at the three bruisers, then at Gertie on the sofa. 'If the boys are caught for something else, they might make a deal and give you up. And Gertie, what about her? She's mad at you for fooling around with Denise.

She might do the dirty on you out of spite. You better think long and hard before you decide to send the club, Leo and myself up in smoke.'

Once again I had to admire my companion in distress, as a muffled 'Leck, not Leo' came from his direction.

Now it was Bertie's turn to gaze at each of the others. 'Can't you see what he's doing?' he said. 'He's playing for time. And also trying to set us against one another. It's an old trick, but it's not going to work here.'

He stood up, his head barely above the surface of the large desk. Then he came out around it, trailing cigar smoke.

'Bring them along,' he ordered. 'We'll stick them in the broom cupboard. Then we'll do what has to be done and get out of here.'

with a grille over it, in the back wall, above our heads. Spiderman might be able to get to it, but not a fourteen stone, over the hill ex-Wexford hurler. No, if we were to get out of there, it would have to be by some other means. And the faster the better, for this time not alone could I smell smoke, but I could see it as it curled in under the door.

## Chapter Seventeen

The sight of the smoke frightened the living daylights out of me. I picked up one of the brushes and threw it like a spear at the high window. The brush missed, then fell back on poor old Leck-Leo's head, adding to the pain he was in already.

I turned my attention to the door, beating on it with my handcuffed hands and shouting for help. I got a nice echo going, but it was only my own voice answering me. The smoke, which had started out as little wisps, was now billowing in, thick and black and choking. I could also hear a crackling noise, and it wasn't Bertie taking the cellophane off another of his cigars. It was obviously the sound of flames eating into the wood and timbers of the nightclub building.

Because my hands were tied in front of me, I was able, finally, to get out of the yellow cape. I wrapped it around my companion, covering his nose and mouth. Then I tore off my shirt and covered my own face with it.

I attacked the door again, kicking at it as hard as I could. When I stopped for breath, to my surprise the kicking sounds continued. Was it the effect of the smoke, or was there someone on the other side, trying to get in? Now why would anyone want to get in when we were so eager to get out? I asked myself. Then the crazy notion came to me that we were being rescued. Some good person was out there, trying to break the door down. My guardian angel, perhaps? Emily, with her toy hammer? Bertie and his goons, after a change of mind? What the hell did it matter, so long as he, she or they managed to get us out?

I put my ear to the panel and heard a voice telling me to get back. I did so, dragging Leck-Leo with me. We stood against the back wall, the room now so full of smoke that it was difficult to see anything.

The thumps on the door became louder. Then, as the smoke suddenly cleared, I saw an axe head appear through one of the panels. It knocked out the top part of the door and, for a moment, I expected the actor Jack Nicholson to stick his head through and shout, 'Here's Johnny'. Instead I could see an even more sinister figure, wearing a crash helmet and holding an axe, peering in.

Whoever he was, he made short work of the rest of the door. He came in, followed by another couple of bikers. They picked up my companion and ran out with him. Then the guy with the axe pushed me along after them.

Flames were licking along the ceiling of the corridor and the heat was terrific. I could feel the skin of my face starting to sizzle. The window by which I had gained entry was now completely smashed. I was pushed from behind through the gaping hole. I fell on my face and rolled about on the wet pavement.

Rain was still falling, hard and steady. I lay on my back and let it soak into me. Never in my life had I been so glad of the showery Irish climate. And never again would I complain about it. Let it pour, spring and summer included!

# Chapter Eighteen

I didn't have much time to roll around on the ground. I was pulled roughly to my feet and pushed down a side street, away from the blazing inferno that had been the Purple Pussy nightclub. My last view of it was of the wooden figure of the cat over the door. It was outlined in flames and falling onto the street below.

The alleyway led to a wide square, where a large van was parked. Stencilled on the side were the words, 'Polonski and Son, Builders and Decorators'. Now the rescue was beginning to make sense. And it became totally clear when the figure with the axe pulled off his helmet, revealing the face and moustache of Abraham Polonski.

'Boy, am I glad to see you,' I told him, grabbing his hand and shaking it vigorously.

'No time for that,' he responded. 'We must get away. The fire brigade, the police, they will all be here soon.'

'Who are those other guys?' I asked him, nodding at his companions. They were in the process of mounting their motor bicycles.

'We Romanians stick together. When one is in trouble, we are all in trouble. I called in my cousins, my uncles, even my father is here. I could not leave you to find Leo alone.'

'You're like the Three Musketeers, all for one and one for all.'

'Enough talk. Get in the van. We will go to our warehouse in Santry. There are things to be done.'

'Leo needs a doctor,' I said, as we both climbed up into the cab of the vehicle. 'He's been badly worked over.'

'They are taking him to hospital as we speak.'

'It was Boyer and his thugs ...'

'I know. That is why we are taking them to my warehouse. They must be punished for their deeds.'

'You've got them? Where are they?'

'In the back of the van. When we arrived, they were escaping down the alleyway beside the club. We will make them very sorry for what they have done.'

Polonski had started up the van as he talked, and we were soon out on the quays and heading north. The roads were clear, and we made good time. In spite of the rain beating against the windscreen and the chill of the air, my face still felt as if it had been lightly toasted under a grill. I opened my mouth and worked my jaws, feeling the skin stretch. I reckon I now know how a lobster feels, when he's thrown into a pot of boiling water.

We journeyed along to the sound of thumps and yells from the back of the van. Bertie and the boys getting their lumps? The thought made me feel much better, and I was in high spirits when we arrived at the Polonskis' warehouse in Santry.

The building was large and well lit inside. Building materials were neatly stacked and there was a sense of order about the place. A stairs led to a glassed-in office, and I could imagine Abraham Polonski sitting up there, keeping an eye on things.

We moved down towards a far corner of the building. Bertie, Gertie and the three thugs were marched along in front of us. The Polonski cousins and uncles all had sallow skin and huge moustaches. There was no doubt that they were related to Abraham. I was introduced to his father, a little dried prune of a man who appeared to have very little English. His moustache was so big that it looked as if he were hiding behind a bush. I wondered if Annie would like me more if I grew whiskers like his. They say you've never been kissed till you've been kissed by a man with a moustache.

# Chapter Nineteen

It took a guy with cutters only a matter of minutes to remove my handcuffs. I admired his skill, but I still counted my fingers when he was finished, just to make sure they were all there.

Bertie and the three thugs were lined up against the wall of the building. A huge can of paint was tied to each of their right ankles to stop them from running away. Gertie was allowed to sit on a stack of wooden planks. It seemed strange to see her with nothing to eat.

Facing them on straight chairs were

tie and company had set fire to
ple Pussy nightclub, with the
i boy and myself still inside.
uld also bear witness that five
d euro was due to the family
ration work.

or my part, said I'd ring
tendent George Quinlan, and
im a version of what had
ed that night. He could then
ith his merry men and collect
ty parties.

e we waited for the police to
the Romanians amused
ves by stripping Bertie and the
oods naked and painting them





the Romanians, like a jury of good men and true. Abraham's father was obviously the judge, for he was placed to one side on a high stool. Would he have the power to give the death sentence if Bertie and his chums were found guilty? The thought made me uneasy. I didn't want to be a party to a lynching. Or maybe a chain-saw blood bath.

'What are you going to do with them?' I asked Abraham, who was standing beside me.

'Get them to admit their guilt. Then punish them.'

'Punish them, how?'

He shrugged and rolled his eyes, as much as to say I'll give you three guesses.

To be fair to Bertie Boyer, he was still game. His suit was torn, his shirt stained, and there was a purple swelling under his right eye. But he had the look of a little bantam cock as he said, 'You guys better let me go and fast. Otherwise my solicitor will sue you for everything you've got. Kidnapping is still illegal in this country, you know.'

'You should have thought of that when you took my son,' Abraham Polonski said. 'And beat him up.'

'Have you any proof that I did that. As I hear it, your son got drunk and fell down. I can't be held responsible for that.'

'Oh yes you can, you little shrimp.' Gertie suddenly spoke up. 'This is payback time for the way you carried on with that Denise. And don't think you were fooling me with talk of it being about business. With her draped around you like a wilted wall flower.'

# Chapter Twenty

It was a week later and Annie, Emily and myself were on our way down to visit the Polonski family in their Parnell Street flat. The rain had finally stopped, and it was a crisp October day with just a hint of winter in its breath. I had used Bertie's two hundred pounds to get my car patched up, but it still coughed and rattled all the way there.

I rang the bell of 49A and stood back. Sure enough, when the door opened the labrador sprang out, ready for battle. Before we left, I had made sure that Emily had her toy rubber hammer. She hit the dog a hefty wallop on the nose with it. That immediately put manners on him. He backed off, his tail between his legs, a look of sorrow in his big brown eyes.

The same old lady, who turned out to be Abraham Polonski's mother, invited us in. The living room was crowded. Father Polonski was there, Abraham and his wife, and a host of uncles, aunts, nephews, nieces and cousins. Leck-Leo introduced me to his partner, Alice, and to their baby son.

'We have named him Patrick, as he was born here in Ireland. He is the first Irish-Romanian in the family.'

We were served hot sweet tea and various types of spicy, garlic sausages. Also dishes of tripe. Annie and I did our best with this food, but Emily showed her displeasure by throwing the tripe at the wall. Later, the women went into an another room and Abraham broke out the rum. In fact, it was Romanian brandy. After a few snorts of it I found myself doing a Cossack dance across the floor.

I don't remember much about the rest of the evening. I know I woke up the next morning feeling that Emily was beating out the Irish national anthem on my head with her rubber hammer.

A few months later I read in the paper that Bertie Boyer had been given five years hard labour for arson and attempted murder.

I lost touch with Gertie, but then, just after Christmas, a card arrived. We were invited to her wedding to one Mircea Petrescu, and I guessed she had hooked up with one of the Romanian moustaches.

As for me, I went back to spying through keyholes and turning over people's dirty laundry. Well, it's a job, and someone has to do it.

## OPEN DOOR SERIES

### SERIES ONE

*Sad Song* by Vincent Banville
*In High Germany* by Dermot Bolger
*Not Just for Christmas* by Roddy Doyle
*Maggie's Story* by Sheila O'Flanagan
*Jesus and Billy Are Off to Barcelona*
by Deirdre Purcell
*Ripples* by Patricia Scanlan

### SERIES TWO

*No Dress Rehearsal* by Marian Keyes
*Joe's Wedding* by Gareth O'Callaghan
*It All Adds Up* by Margaret Neylon
*Second Chance* by Patricia Scanlan
*Pipe Dreams* by Anne Schulman
*Old Money, New Money* by Peter Sheridan

### SERIES THREE

*An Accident Waiting to Happen*
by Vincent Banville
*The Builders* by Maeve Binchy
*Letter From Chicago* by Cathy Kelly
*Driving With Daisy* by Tom Nestor
*The Comedian* by Joseph O'Connor
*Has Anyone Here Seen Larry?*
by Deirdre Purcell